K-77	DATE DUE	
FE 81		
P82		
P82		
BS		
H1		

Little Mops at the Seashore

By Elzbieta

Doubleday & Company, Inc.,
Garden City, New York

For Barbara

ISBN: 0-385-06792-5 Trade
        0-385-02654-4 Prebound

Library of Congress Catalog Card Number 73-10375

Copyright (c) 1972 by George Allen & Unwin Ltd.

Printed in the United States of America

First Edition

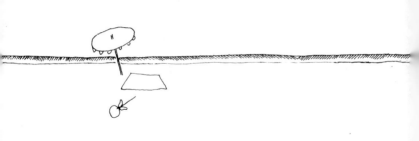

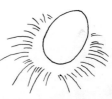

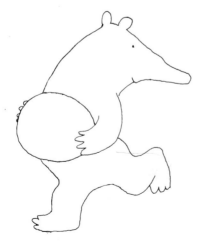

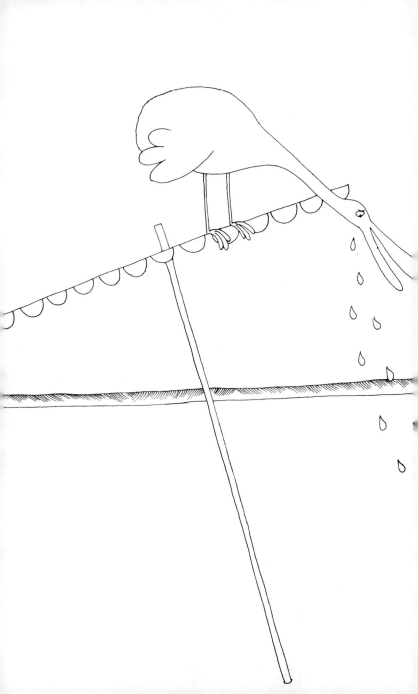